CLEOPATRA BONES

AND THE
GOLDEN CHIMPANZEE

Cleopatra Bones

Al McNasty

Ringo and Ramona Lamarr

Jumping Jack O'Malley

Leo Longclaw

Diego Del Grippo

Jango Karbunkel

Ella Egghart

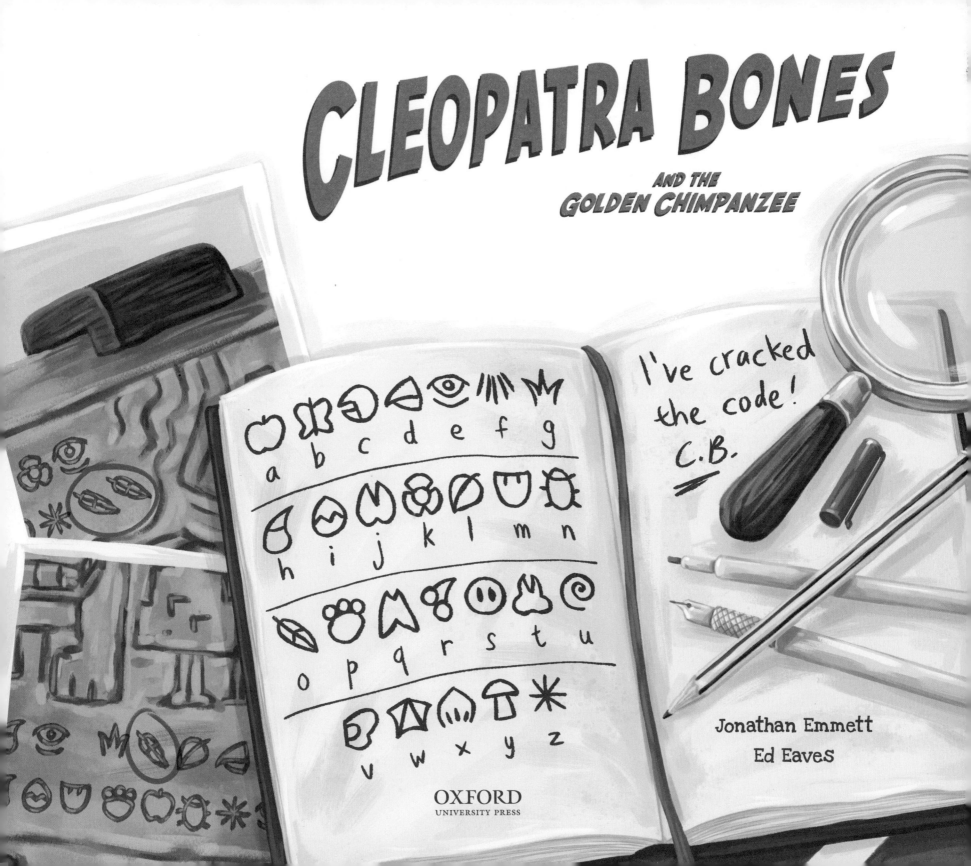

In the ruins of a temple,
down a dark and winding stair,
explorer Cleopatra Bones is
creeping with great care.

Springing nimbly sideways
to avoid a deadly trap . . .

. . . she squeezes through a secret door and finds a TREASURE MAP!

Back at the museum,
the experts all agree,
the map shows the location of
THE GOLDEN CHIMPANZEE.

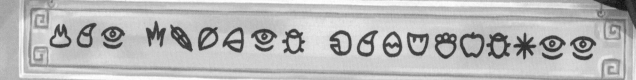

A priceless, precious statue, or so the stories say,
but no one knew its whereabouts—at least until today.

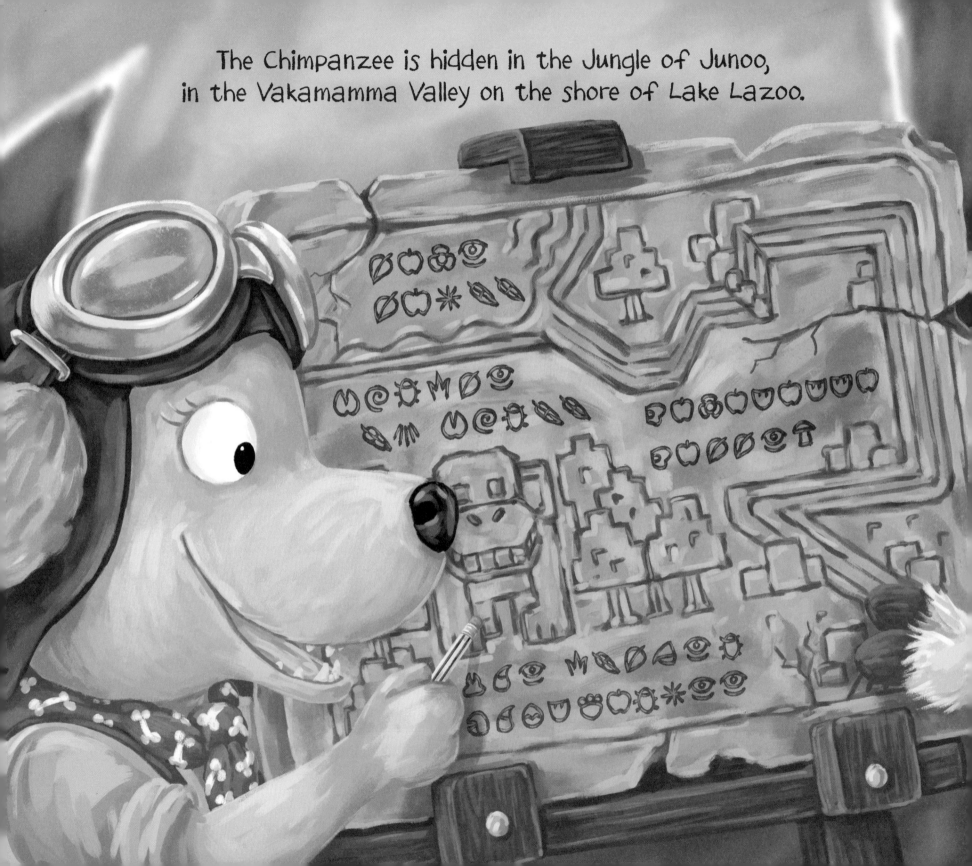

The Chimpanzee is hidden in the Jungle of Junoo,
in the Vakamamma Valley on the shore of Lake Lazoo.

Everyone's excited that
the secret's out at last.

But the news is spreading
quickly, so they'd better
get there FAST.

Speeding up the river, the first to reach the valley
is the famous frog adventurer Jumping Jack O'Malley.

Built to stand the sharpest blows, the heaviest of knocks,
Jack's rugged rapids-racer goes crashing through the rocks.

Next, the valley echoes with a noisy whirring sound
as Leo Longclaw's jungle-copter lowers to the ground.

Before the copter's landed,
Leo's bounded out the door,
and plunged into the jungle
with a treasure-hungry roar.

Cleopatra Bones arrives by powered parachute. The others see her circling round and set off in pursuit.

Something on the ground below has clearly caught her eye.
And whatever she is heading for, they want to be nearby.

It's a massive monkey statue, overlooked and overgrown.
It's certainly a chimpanzee, but this one's made of STONE.

So the quest continues, but the searchers don't go far,
before they're interrupted by . . .

. . . an armoured aqua-car!

The aqua-car skids to a stop beside the statue's feet.
And out springs Al McNasty, that greedy, grasping cheat!

Al's sure he knows just where the missing treasure can be found.
He's certain that the chimpanzee is buried underground.

But Al is much too lazy
to go digging with a spade.
Why dig a hole by hand when
there's a fortune to be made?

And it would take forever, why he might be there all night.
So Al intends to BLAST A HOLE with sticks of DYNAMITE!

The valley echoes as this awful alligator
pushes down the plunger and creates a massive crater.
There's lots of dirt and rubble, but to Al's immense displeasure,
there's no sign of the Golden Chimp or any other treasure!

The blast wave shook the valley
and behind Al's scaly back,
the ancient statue splits apart
with an almighty crack.

And then, before McNasty has the time to turn around, the statue's bottom falls on him and pins him to the ground.

And from the broken body pours a waterfall of gold,
a glittering, glistening torrent that's a wonder to behold.

It seems that this stone statue WAS the treasure that they sought.
But it's golden on the INSIDE, not the outside as they'd thought.

There's gold enough for everyone to have an ample share,
so Cleopatra and the others split it, fair and square.

And everybody celebrates their great discovery,
it once was lost, but now it's found—

THE GOLDEN CHIMPANZEE!

For Alexis and Kristian—J.E

For Becs, my co-pilot xx—E.E

OXFORD
UNIVERSITY PRESS

Great Clarendon Street, Oxford OX2 6DP

Oxford University Press is a department of the University of Oxford.
It furthers the University's objective of excellence in research, scholarship,
and education by publishing worldwide. Oxford is a registered trade mark of
Oxford University Press in the UK and in certain other countries

Text copyright © Jonathan Emmett 2018
Illustration copyright © Ed Eaves 2018

The moral rights of the author and artist have been asserted

Database right Oxford University Press (maker)

First published 2018

British Library Cataloguing in Publication Data available

ISBN: 978-0-19-276737-0

1 3 5 7 9 10 8 6 4 2

Printed in China

Paper used in the production of this book is a natural, recyclable product made
from wood grown in sustainable forests. The manufacturing process conforms
to the environmental regulations of the country of origin

Find out more about Jonathan Emmett's books at
scribblestreet.co.uk

And discover more of Ed Eaves' books at
edeavesillustrator.com

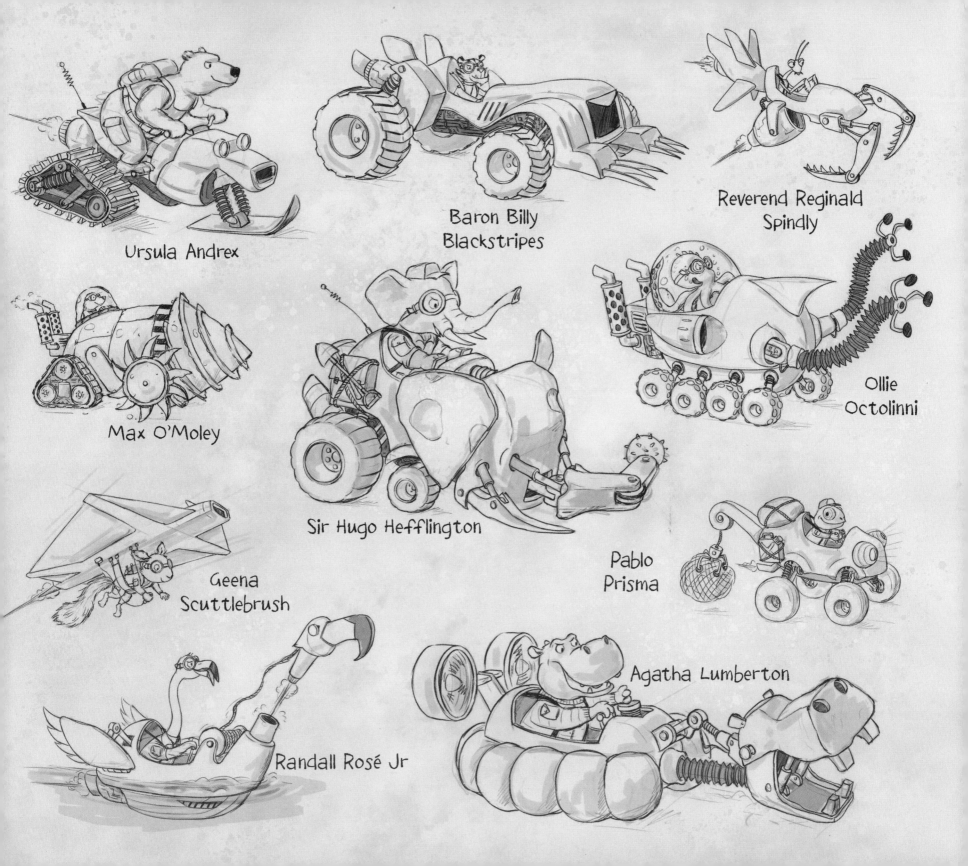

Ursula Andrex

Baron Billy
Blackstripes

Reverend Reginald
Spindly

Max O'Moley

Sir Hugo Hefflington

Ollie
Octolinni

Geena
Scuttlebrush

Pablo
Prisma

Randall Rosé Jr

Agatha Lumberton